Super Pooper!

Author: Monika Sloan
Illustration: Mike Motz
Design: Jason Fain

**This book is dedicated to my sons
Jarod and Brady.**

Hi!
My name is Jarod.

**I am going to tell you
the story about how
I became a
super pooper.**

When I was a little baby,
I used to pee and poop
in my diaper.

Then when I got a
little older and a little bigger,
I learned to pee in the potty
all by myself!

It wasn't long after that when
I learned to poop in the potty
all by myself!

My mommy was so proud of me
she said I was a
super pooper.

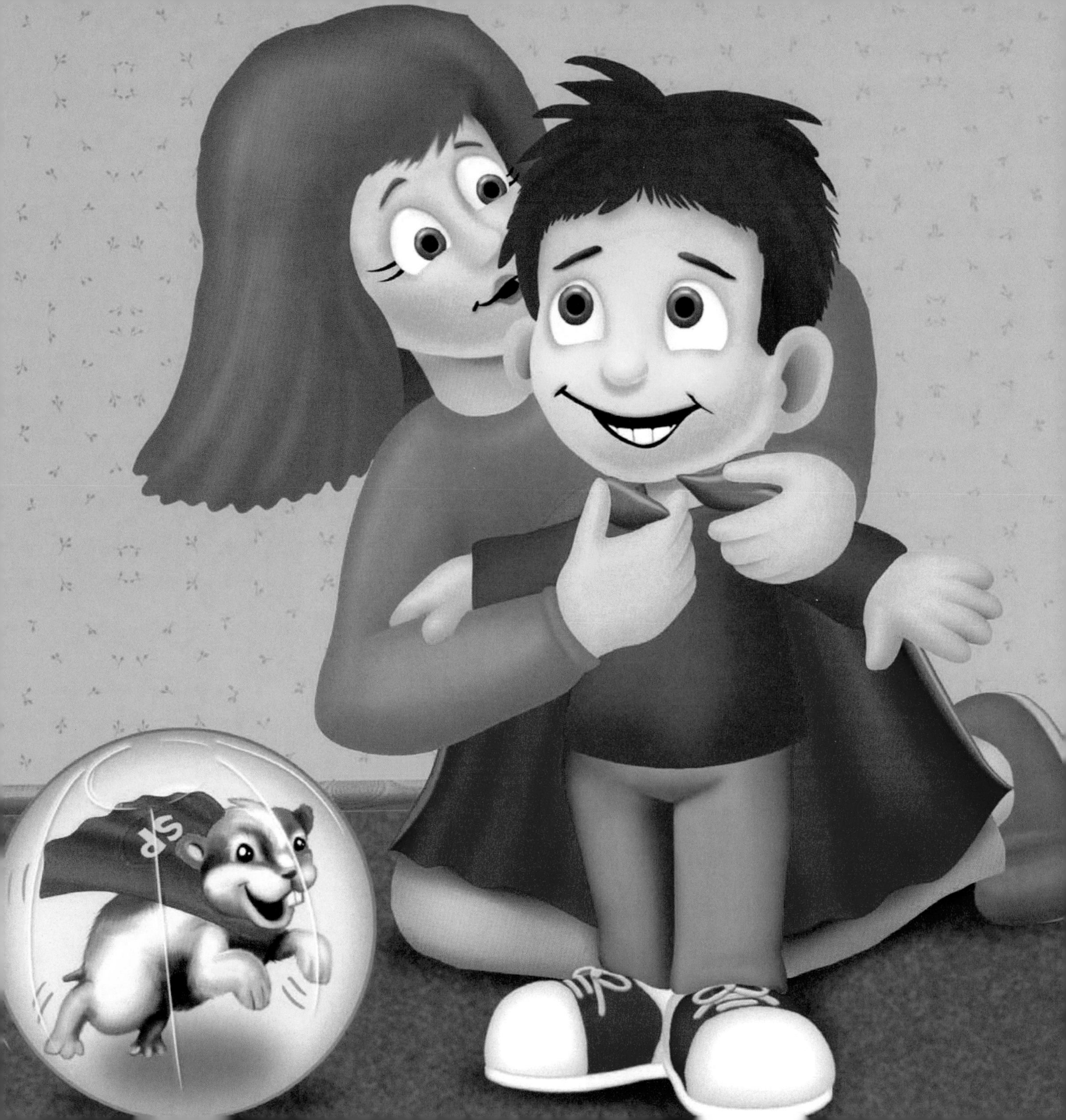

We had a very fun party
just for me.

I wore a special
super pooper crown
and cape.

I like being a super pooper.
I don't need diapers any more.

I even get to wear big boy
underwear. I have a cool pair
with race cars on them.

After I poop in the potty
I always remember to
wash my hands.

Being a super pooper is
fun and important.

Now I am going to teach my
little brother how to poop in
the potty so he can become a
super pooper like me.

So that is the story
of how I became a
super pooper.

I hope you can become
a super pooper too.

Monika Sloan is a nurse and mother of two.

"I know how frustrating potty training can be.
The best thing you can do is to have patience.
Keep things positive and fun. It will happen.
You can do it!"

44212974R00015

Made in the USA
Middletown, DE
31 May 2017